# Panda's New Toy

For Stephen Fry
J. D.

For Nat, who likes toys
H. C.

Text copyright © 1999 by Joyce Dunbar
Illustrations copyright © 1999 by Helen Craig

First U.S. edition 1999

Library of Congress Cataloging-in-Publication Data

Dunbar, Joyce.
Panda's new toy / written by Joyce Dunbar ; illustrated by Helen Craig.
— 1st U.S. ed.
p.    cm. — (Panda and Gander stories)
Summary: When Panda gets a new toy, he wants to play with it himself and
doesn't want to give Gander a turn.
ISBN 0-7636-0724-X
[1. Selfishness — Fiction.  2. Play — Fiction.  3. Pandas — Fiction.
4. Geese — Fiction.]  I. Craig, Helen, ill.  II. Title.
III. Series: Dunbar, Joyce.  Panda and Gander stories.
PZ7.D8944Pan    1999
[E] — dc21    98-14045

10 9 8 7 6 5 4 3 2 1

Printed in Hong Kong

This book was typeset in AT Arta.
The pictures were done in watercolor and line.

Candlewick Press
2067 Massachusetts Avenue
Cambridge, Massachusetts 02140

# Panda's
# New Toy

## Joyce Dunbar

### illustrated by
## Helen Craig

CANDLEWICK PRESS
CAMBRIDGE, MASSACHUSETTS

Panda had a new toy.

It was a cup and a ball.

The ball was fastened

to the cup with

a piece of string.

"How do you play with it?"

asked Gander.

"The game is to swing the ball and catch it in the cup," said Panda.

"I'll show you."

Panda swung the ball and . . .

missed.

# He swung it again and . . .

## missed again!

He swung it and missed,

again . . .

and again.

"Can I have a turn?" asked
Gander.

"Wait until I do it right,"
said Panda.

Panda swung the ball again . . .

and caught it!

"See, Gander. I caught the ball in the cup. That's what you have to do."

"Just watch again."

Panda swung the ball . . .

and missed!

But then he swung it and

caught it,

again . . .

and again.

"Can I have a turn now?" asked Gander.

"It might be too hard for you,"
  said Panda.

"It looks easy," said Gander.

"It's easy for me," said Panda.

"So easy I think I could catch it
  with my eyes closed. Let's see."

Panda swung the ball and caught
it with his eyes closed.

"Is it my turn now?" asked Gander.
"I think I could even catch it
 standing on one leg," said Panda.
"Watch this."

So Panda swung the ball and
caught it standing on one leg.
"That's good,"

said Gander.

"Is it my turn now?"

"I want to see if I can eat a cookie
with one paw and catch the ball
with the other," said Panda.

Panda ate a cookie with one paw
and caught the ball with the other.

"Now it's my turn," said Gander.
"First I want to see if I can swing
on the swing and still catch the ball
in the cup," said Panda.

So Gander pushed
Panda on the
swing . . .

while Panda caught the
ball in the cup.
"I think I could be an acrobat,"
said Panda.

"I think you could," said Gander,

"but it's my turn now."

"I'll just have one last turn,"

said Panda.

"You've had lots of last turns,"

said Gander.

"A really last turn," said Panda.

So Panda had a really last turn.

But he swung the ball too hard and

broke the string!

Away rolled the ball.

Gander went running to catch it.

"Now I won't be able to have
a turn," said Gander.
"Yes, you will," said Panda.
And he tied a knot in the string
so that the ball was attached to
the cup again.

"Good," said Gander.

"Now can I have a turn?"

"Let me see if it works first,"
said Panda. "The string might be
too long or too short."

"Panda," said Gander.

"What is it?" said Panda.

"I don't care if the string is too
long or too short.

I don't want to play with that toy anymore. I'm going to play with the jolly trolley."

"Gander," said Panda.

"What is it?" said Gander.

"It's your turn with the cup and the ball. I want to play with the jolly trolley."

"Good," said Gander to Panda, "because it's my turn to ride on the jolly trolley and your turn to pull it along."

And riding along on the jolly trolley, Gander swung the ball in the cup and—

caught it!